THIS EDITION PUBLISHED BY PARRAGON BOOKS LTD IN 2014

PARRAGON BOOKS LTD
CHARTIST HOUSE
15-17 TRIM STREET
BATH BA1 1HA, UK
WWW.PARRAGON.COM

EDITED BY MICHAEL DIGGLE
DESIGNED BY ALEX DIMOND
PRODUCTION BY RICHARD WHEELER

ISBN 978-1-4723-6466-1

PRINTED IN CHINA

T-REX TERROR

THE SUPERSAURUS LEGEND BEGINS...

WRITTEN BY
TIMOTHY KNAPMAN

ILLUSTRATED BY
TIM WESSON

Parragon

Bath • New York • Cologne • Melbourne • Delhi
Hong Kong • Shenzhen • Singapore • Amsterdam

65 million years ago...

A radioactive meteorite hurtles through outer space, heading straight for planet Earth...

And the bustling dinotropolis of New Dino City!

IS IT A PTERODACTYL?

IS IT A PLANE?

ARE WE GOING TO BECOME EXTINCT?

Meanwhile, in Cretaceous Park, four young dinos are playing dinoball, but their lives are about to CHANGE FOR EVER!

As the dust settles, Terra begins to cough.

Suddenly, out bursts...

A BLAZING FIREBALL!

COUGH!

It bounces off an...

UNBREAKABLE FORCE FIELD!

It's punched away by...

UNBEATABLE STRENGTH!

And it's finally dodged by...

UNBELIEVABLE STRETCH!

The four friends walk home, full of questions...

Suddenly, from a nearby bank, they hear a cry for...

It's another Raptor robbery! But if those pesky predators think they'll get away THIS time, they're in for a SUPER surprise...

And in that electrifying moment, the LEGEND begins!

In no time, the SUPERSAURS are the talk of New Dino City...

ANOTHER CRIME FOILED!
Criminals car-n't believe it!

The Daily Reptile · NEW DINO CITY

MAYOR OPENS HI-TECH SUPERSAURUS HQ!

"Honest Al" Allosaur, Mayor of NDC, says "City safe with the Supersaurs!"

NEW DINO CITY SWOOPERS SIGN DOC
New signing to STRETCH Swooper winning streak.

Before long, the Supersaurs have rid New Dino City of crime and things are all quiet at Supersaurus HQ.

Doc loves his gadgets, but there's something not quite right about this giveaway...

Back at Supersaurus HQ, Trix is monitoring the bay around
New Dino City. He's picked up some movement on Volcano Island.

When suddenly every
monitor is tuned to...

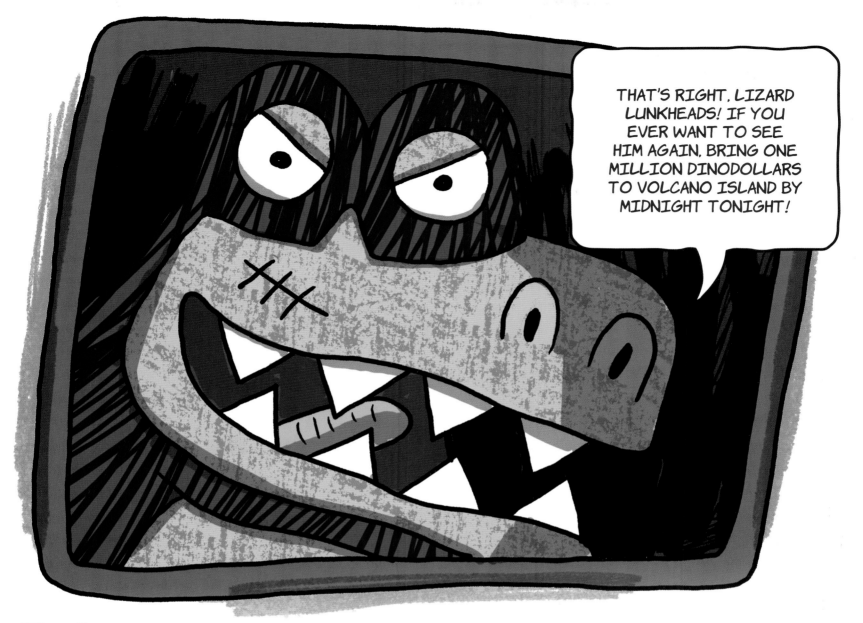

The Supersaurs spring into action!

Oh, no! Is this the end for the Supersaurs?

No trap can hold the Supersaurs!

In no time at all the Supersaurs are inside...

But T-Rex isn't beaten yet!

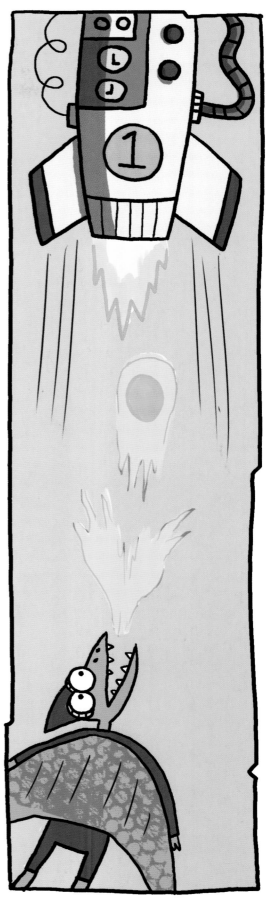

Can Terra stop the rocket in time?

With only seconds to spare, Terra's fireball smashes the rocket out of the sky!

And so the city is safe... until next time!